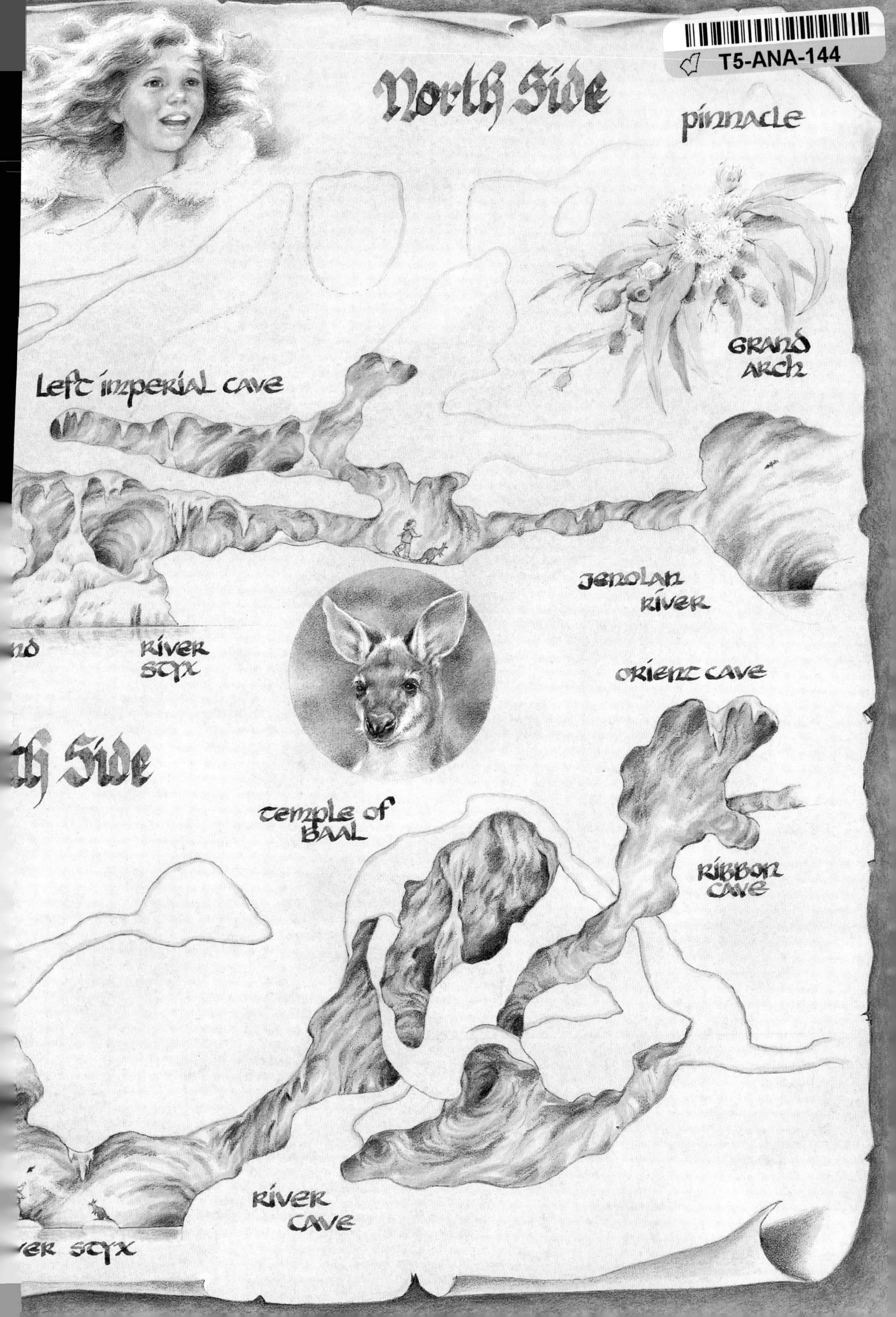

North Side

pinnacle

GRAND ARCH

Left imperial cave

JENOLAN RIVER

RIVER STYX

ORIENT CAVE

th Side

temple of BAAL

RIBBON CAVE

RIVER CAVE

ER STYX

Caves House, JENOLAN CAVES

The Wizard of Jenolan

ISBN 0 646 14427 8

THE WIZARD of JENOLAN

CONTENTS

CHAPTER 1
"Something"

Thel had been asleep - or perhaps she hadn't been. But now, suddenly, she was sitting straight up in bed, almost seeing her own whisper creeping out across the moonlit room with little shuffling footsteps -

"Elsie! Are you - are you awake, Elsie?"

But no, Elsie was not awake. What with the long journey to Caves House in this valley of Jenolan, and the change of air, and all the mountain scenery, and having her young cousin to look after, she had fallen fast asleep.

So Thel didn't say any more, but sat quite still for a long time, listening and thinking. And the strange thing was that something else seemed to be listening, too - in a waiting sort of way. Or was she just imagining?

She remembered her Uncle Peter saying, with that nice smile of his, "You've got an imagination twice as big as *you* are, young lady."

But also, she remembered the bus trip here this afternoon, and the strange feeling she'd had that things were not quite as they seemed . . . that the hills encircling this valley, for instance, were actually giants sitting in a huge ring, talking about something frightfully important, with all their knees together.

And now, this strange Something that seemed to be listening the same as she was - what could it possibly be?

Apart from Elsie's breathing, there wasn't a sound in the room, and nothing unusual to be seen, either - only moonlight.

"So perhaps that's what it is," Thel told herself. "Moonlight." But somehow, she knew that it wasn't.

Anyway, she was too tired to keep wondering about it right now, so she slipped down under the bedclothes again, and would have gone straight off to sleep only that, just outside her window, there was a little watery-sounding voice chuckling away to itself.

And every now and then, a bird snipped open the silence with a single note, like the chime of a goblin clock. ("Uncle Peter was right. I do keep imagining things, don't I?" she thought, drowsily.)

And there were lots of small flutterings in the huge tree just outside her window, as birds ruffled themselves and turned in their sleep. Strangest of all - again and again there was a little tumbling and clattering sound, over the asphalt pathway down below.

And Thel was still trying to work out what this might be when, at last, she fell asleep.

CHAPTER 2
Discoveries

The next morning, it seemed to Thel that there was something very special about everything - even about the dining-room, with all of its shiny cutlery and snow-white tables, each surrounded by nicely dressed people who used their serviettes and spoke politely.

But then, one of the ladies at Thel's table asked her, "Are you visiting a cave this morning, dear?" And suddenly, all of the "special" feeling that she'd had about everything vanished, as she answered, unhappily, "No, I'm afraid not."

"Oh dear, I feel such a spoil-sport!" her cousin explained, smiling apologetically. "But the truth is, she's been quite ill, you see - and Doctor gave very strict instructions: nothing strenuous for at least a fortnight."

"Oh well, in that case . . ." the lady replied, obviously meaning that there was no further argument.

"The point is," said Thel, frowning at the seriousness of it.

"Yes, dear?" the lady prompted.

"Well, there are all those wonderful caves, right underneath where we're sitting."

"Yes, some of them would be, no doubt."

"And there's a stuffy old doctor in Sydney, with spectacles halfway down his nose, saying that I can't see them. Do you think that's fair?"

For some strange reason, everyone around the table thought that that was something to laugh or smile at.

But, with breakfast over at last, Thel wandered outside into the warm sunshine - and everything was glad again.

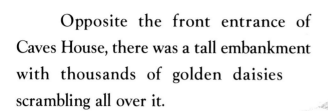

Opposite the front entrance of
Caves House, there was a tall embankment
with thousands of golden daisies
scrambling all over it.

Then, a pair of blue-and-
crimson rosellas got into a flustering
discussion about something, in the
tree above her, and knocked down a soft
green ball, which split open as it hit the asphalt
- and out spun a walnut, of all things, in its hard little
hollow-sounding shell.

Thel pounced after it, but it had no intention of being
caught, and went tumbling off at a great rate, until it landed in a
bed of stinging nettles.

Thel stood peering at it for a moment, realizing what it was that had
clattered along the path so many times during the night - then went back and
looked high up into the first walnut-tree she had ever seen.

And right there, trilling away behind the tree, was the little chuckling voice
she had heard in the night - coming from a trickle of water with a tiny bridge
standing over it.

"But I still don't know about that something else, do I?" she asked
herself, softly.

"What something else?" asked a voice right behind her.

Thel turned quickly, and found herself looking into the brightest eyes she had ever seen. And underneath the eyes, there was an impishly crooked, smiling mouth, with streaks of gold glistening. And all of these belonged to a raggedy-looking little woman, leaning forward over a rail, with her hands clasped under her chin, and a brightly coloured rosella perched on her shoulder, contentedly nibbling at a slice of apple.

Thel stared wide-eyed for a moment, then suddenly smiled.

"Oh, that's heaps better!" exclaimed Billy the Bird Woman - for that was what the wild creatures called her.

Then, leaning forward still nearer, she added in a hushed voice, "But now, you really must let me take a swallow-dive into that secret of yours - because it *is* a secret, isn't it? - and it sounds delicious."

"Delicious?" Thel repeated, uncertainly.

"Yes, yes - like honey and strawberry ice-cream, sprinkled with rainbow."

Thel smiled. She had never before met anyone like this. But then, she had never before felt the way she had last night about that mysterious Something, either. And it occurred to her now that the two of them might somehow be connected. So she said, "Well actually, that's just it. It *is* a secret - from me, as well. I haven't the slightest idea what it was. Just a funny sort of Something that seemed to be in my room last night."

"Ah!" said Billy, flashing a quick glance at her. "That's important - very, very important. You must make sure you remember it."

"But how can I remember it if I don't know what it is?"

The sparkle in Billy's eyes darted away from Thel to the top of a tree . . . to a flying lorikeet . . . to the scampering of a young wallaby.

"And what good would it do if I did remember whatever it is, anyway?" Thel added.

"I don't know," said Billy. "Nobody does. That's just the point. Anything might happen. Don't forget, now!"

Then, with a shiver of excitement and a jingling of bracelets, she turned and flitted off down the broad pathway with tiny footsteps that scarcely touched the ground.

Thel stood gazing after her, feeling more puzzled than ever, and also feeling sure that, as Billy the Bird Woman had said, anything could happen now. Just anything.

CHAPTER 3
The Blue Lake

Only a short walk away from Caves House, there was a giant cavern called the Grand Arch. It was here that people gathered together every morning, afternoon and evening, ready for a guide to lead them underground into one of the caves, and -

"Oh, come on, Elsie - please!" Thel said, once again.

But no. Her cousin insisted they were the last places that anyone just better from a serious illness should go to.

"Don't be silly, Thel!" she said. "And don't keep making me feel bad about not taking you! They're cold and damp and slippery and full of steps. Right?"

So Thel didn't say any more about it from then on, because she loved Elsie, and had no wish to bother her. But that made no difference whatever to the way she felt about it herself.

Many times a day, she would wander off to scramble among the rocks in the Grand Arch. And this was always exciting, for there were lots of tiny hollows hidden away there, and sometimes rocky towers and castles just big enough for gnomes to live in - only funny little spiders were living there instead. And for some reason, it seemed rather strange, finding spiders and their webs amongst rocks instead of branches. Also, there were swarms of frisky wallabies, who sprang about among the little caverns, stopping to gaze at her with sharp, inquisitive eyes.

And just beyond the Grand Arch there was the Blue Lake, where a few stately swans and crowds of playful little ducks lived.

Thel made a point of hurrying down there in the early mornings, to feed them when they were hungriest, before the man in uniform came along with whole bucketfuls of scraps.

The Blue Lake itself was as blue as its name, with willow-trees all around, trailing their branches in it, like long green fingers. And often, if you looked hard enough, you could see big white duck eggs hidden away in secret places among the willows. Most wonderful of all, the water in it came from the world inside the hills. The Blue Lake out here, was the River Styx in the caves. And Thel never went visiting the Lake without trying to imagine what that great underground world might look like.

Today, for a few moments, she had been standing quite still on the shores of the Blue Lake when she realized that everything else seemed very still too, and very silent, and that there was the oddest feeling of something else, like the Something in her room that first night. Something that the whole of Nature was standing in awe of.

Even the little Blue Lake ducks had stopped their pecking, plunging and flapping, and were gliding up together quietly, as though watching and listening for something that was just about to happen.

But at that very moment, a soft cooee sounded from the embankment above her, and Thel looked up to see Billy the Bird Woman twinkling down at her - with, as usual, a blue-and-crimson rosella balancing on her shoulder.

"Has anything happened yet?" Billy asked, a trifle breathlessly.

"No," Thel replied, in a loud whisper. "But I do believe it was just going to."

"Ah!" said Billy, glancing sideways. "That's very important. You must be sure to remember it."

"But," Thel complained, "that's just like it was before. I still don't know what it is, so how can I remember it?"

"Yes, yes, I see what you mean. But if you do keep remembering, I'm sure you'll find out what it is pretty soon."

Thel considered this carefully, then frowned. "But that's back-to-front and upside-down," she said.

"Only because you don't stand on your head or wear your eyes behind you," the little Bird Woman pointed out.

Reasonably enough, Thel asked, "What good would it do if I did?"

"Well - let's say - it would come in very handy if your Something were an upside-down or a back-to-front sort of Something."

"But - is it?" Thel asked, feeling sure that Billy knew a great deal more than she was telling.

Which might or might not have been true because, instead of answering, Billy wriggled her shoulders up so suddenly that her rosella, with an indignant screech, went flying off to the top of the flagpole.

"Dear, dear, dear!" she muttered. "Oh dear, dear, dear!" And off she went, skimming out of sight, to the jingling of twenty-seven bracelets.

"She's quite the funniest person I've ever met," Thel told herself, then wandered round towards the Grand Arch again.

Wallabies, rocks, echoes, memories, secrets - the arch was full of them. But most wonderful of all was the fact that, on either side, it led away into the untold magic of the caves themselves.

Thel stood gazing at the little signposts pointing in different directions toward the Lucas Cave, the River, Temple of Baal, Orient, Imperial, Ribbon, Jubilee - all of them such wonderful, exciting names. Then, a group of people started coming down the broad roadway.

Soon, the Grand Arch was ringing with the echoes of their voices and footsteps. And oh, if only she could have been one of them! For of course, they were all gathering here ready to visit a cave, as soon as a guide came along to show them the way.

Thel wondered if, this time, he might be the White Star Man, who had often spoken to her, and who was the chief of all the guides. He wore a smart navy-blue uniform, and a cap, and clinging onto each of his lapels with all their pointers, as if they were alive, were small white stars.

Then, just as she was thinking of him, a deep, soft voice spoke into her ear.

"Not coming with me yet, lassie?" And there he was, smiling down at her.

"No - no!" she said - and hurried away before anyone could see how upset she was.

CHAPTER 4
Mister Tite

Suddenly, a large wallaby thudded out from among the rocks, and stood in front of her, perfectly still except for a twitching nose. And, just as suddenly, Thel stood perfectly still, too.

"Oh Wally!" she murmured softly. "I'm sorry - I haven't got any breakfast for you. I gave it all to the ducks."

But, instead of hopping away again when he heard this, he stayed exactly where he was, calmly blinking up at her. He even let her stroke the top of his head - which none of the other wallabies had ever done.

"What a darling you are!" she said. "Look - you wait right here, while I go back to Caves House and see what I can find for you. A nice bit of toast, perhaps."

But when she started to move away, he hopped round in front of her, so that she couldn't go any farther without treading on him. Then, quickly, he glanced several times from Thel to the rocks he had come from, and back to Thel again, with his tiny front feet quivering excitedly.

"Wally dear, what are you trying to say?" she asked.

He answered by hopping off among the rocks, then stopping and looking back to see if Thel was following him. And, without pausing to wonder whether she should or not, she did start following him, step by hop.

Slowly at first, then faster and faster, he led on around narrow, twisting pathways that Thel had never seen before.

"Who ever heard of playing follow-the-leader with a wallaby?" she asked herself. "What on Earth would Elsie think? Elsie!" she repeated aloud, looking about her and realizing how lost she was already, and how worried her cousin would be if she didn't get back soon.

"Wally, stop! Stop!" she called out. "Where are you going? Where are we? I - I can't do this. I'll have to go back!"

For a moment, Wally seemed to be listening to her.

But then, tossing his head, he bounded off into what looked to be a great, black tunnel. And, because he was the only living thing around, Thel bounded after him.

Only to
find that the tunnel
wasn't so dark after all - that there
was actually a very soft light
spreading through it, like a blush.

Even so, it was hard work
keeping up with Wally, who went leaping
over huge rocks as easily as flying, while
Thel could only scramble after him, in too
much of a flurry to watch carefully where
she was going - until, with a thud, she
landed full-length on a rock which turned
out to be a long, steep slippery-slide.

Down she
rushed, with nothing to
grab on to, and no hope of
stopping - until she plunged feet-
first into a very cold and very wet pool.

She would have screamed, only the shock of
coldness took her breath away, and, she nearly sank with
fright - yet somehow waved and splashed and tumbled herself
afloat again. It was only then that she began to hear a strange sort
of laughing voice, deep and echoing, like a gong.

"Come, come! What's all the fuss about ... about ... about?"

"Help!" Thel gasped breathlessly. "I'm d-d-drowning!" Then
choked, spluttered and gurgled over another mouthful of icy water.

"Oh, you want to get *out*, do you? Why didn't you say so ... so ... so?"

And now, as she still kept threshing around, Thel was more
startled than ever to see something big and white, spreading over the
water towards her.

"Oh no!" she cried out.

"Why not?" answered another voice, right beside her - a
ripply-sounding one this time. "I'm only a reflection, anyway.
The master's up on the roof."

But Thel was too frightened and cold and wet to try
to work this out. All she knew was that the whiteness
in the water was all around her now, even sliding
underneath, and gently swivelling her to a part
where she could actually scramble out on to
solid ground.

"Th-thank you very much," she stammered timidly, peering back into the water. And there - shaking with laughter, and crumpling up like a concertina - was an extraordinary creature, with a face and nothing else. No legs, arms, tail, wings, antlers, or even fins.

Then she realized with amazement that - just like magic - she was as warm and dry as she had been cold and wet only a moment ago.

"But of course you are," boomed the voice - with - an - echo - like - a - gong, as though she had spoken instead of only thinking. And it sounded so near to her, that she jumped with yet another fright. "Why *wouldn't* you be dry, now that you're not in the water any longer ... onger ... onger?"

Thel quickly looked up - and there, the same as in the water, was a strange, finless, armless, wingless creature. But solid like rock instead of twisting and crinkling. Beautiful white rock, shaped like an ice-cream cone, with sparkles all over it. And, with a face at the end of him instead of at his top, he was grinning down at her.

"Upon my calcium," he boomed, "you're a queer kind of reflection ... ection ... ection!"

"Oh - no," Thel answered, as politely as possible. "I'm not any kind of reflection. I'm Thel."

"What? Not a reflection? Then what were you doing in the water?"

"I slipped and fell into it."

"Fell! Oh my carbonated calcium! Has there been another earthquake?"

"Not that I know of," said Thel.

"I shouldn't think so. Not when the last one was only a few million years ago ... ago ... ago. Poor old Lucas would go into a premature landslide."

Thinking to herself, Thel wondered if he meant Lucas Cave. And she also very much wondered who he himself was.

"You don't know who I am? I? Stalactite ... tite ... tite?" bellowed the echoing gong, indignantly.

"I'm sorry," Thel said, rather timidly. "It's just that - I've never met anyone like you before. Do you always - well, I mean, do you always wear your face at the end of you like that, instead of at the top?"

And she was remembering what Billy the Bird Woman had said about an upside-downish sort of Something, when suddenly the gong boomed out again, "So I'm upside-down, am I? Just because I'm different ... ifferent ... ifferent!"

And a large drop of water, like a tear, tumbled down his face into the pool below, tickling his reflection into a squirming fit of giggles.

But Stalactite was not amused - and another drop splashed down into the water. "Here I am," he wailed, "working hard every thousand years of my life, building myself into one of the best-looking stalactites in Jenolan - and a Thel sort of person calls me upside-down ... down ... down!"

"Oh, please don't cry, Mr-Mr Tite" - which was all that Thel could remember of the long name he had given himself. "Wrong-way round suits you. It really does," she added politely.

Then, before he could gong out his answer to that, there was a great commotion, with noise and movement everywhere, with shuffling footsteps and dozens of human voices. Sudden lights came on - and Thel's special friend, the White Star Man, stepped on to a little bridge over the reflection pool, with a crowd of cave visitors following him.

"Hullo!" Thel called out excitedly, running up to him. "Hullo, Mr Star Man! Look - here I am! I did get here, after all!"

But he made no sign of hearing her - which was very puzzling indeed. And, even though she started wedging her way amongst the visitors, nobody took the slightest notice of her. Instead, they were all listening intently to what their guide was telling them, and looking around at this and that as he shone extra light on to it with his torch.

This, quite easily, was the scariest thing so far.

"Hullo, everyone!" she called out again, her voice trembling a little. "I'm Thel!"

But nobody answered, and the White Star Man just went on explaining about things like stalactites: how they were formed by water droplets, seeping one by one through limestone, out there in the world above the caves.

"And before they finally drop on to the ground - or, as here, into water - they leave the tiniest particle of lime behind them - "

"Look at me, somebody!" Thel shouted.

"- and that's how stalactites have been formed, down through aeons of time - and are continuing to be formed."

"So, how ever old would these caves be?" one of the visitors asked.

The guide hesitated for a moment, then - looking at Mr Tite - said, "This handsome stalactite, for instance, would have been growing for hundreds of thousands of years."

And everyone gasped, marvelling. Even Thel did, forgetting for a moment that she didn't seem to be anybody anywhere. Yet the Star Man had spoken as though it were quite natural.

In fact, there was something about him which made Thel feel as though he belonged more comfortably down here in the caves than in the ordinary world of shops and houses and cars and roadways.

So she hurried over to him and gripped her fingers around one of his hands. And he actually seemed to feel something, for he looked down at his hand, frowning, and giving it a little stretch - but then, just lifted it up to work the light-switch.

"All right - on a bit farther," he said, leading off down a softly-lit pathway, with everyone following him.

Soon, they had all disappeared into the distance - and Thel was feeling very much alone in this great under-world of the caves, when suddenly something nudged against her, and somebody said,

"Zell, you *ished* to crum nere, fidn't you?" - and there was Wally, with a cheeky look in his eyes as they swivelled now to the right, now to the left.

Thel stared and blinked at him. "What, Wally? Was that you speaking? Sort of speaking?" she added.

Wally jerked his head sideways - which could have meant yes, and could have meant no.

"Well, if it *was* you, that's the very first time you've spoken to me."

"Trisn't! You taven't been rissning."

Thel burst out laughing. "Oh my goodness! That's like a code or something. But I can understand you all right, Wally. And I *have* been listening - and you *haven't* spoken until now, and that's that!"

Even as she was saying this, however, her eyes kept straining to see into what looked like a great darkness that she hadn't noticed before. Then, without being able to help it, she started slowly walking towards it, wondering.

And the nearer she came to it, the colder she began to feel, as though the darkness itself were reaching icy fingers out towards her.

CHAPTER 5
River Styxies

"Trel - crop it! Crum dack!" Wally commanded, with a crackle in his voice.

But she took no notice, as though indeed, once again, she hadn't heard him, and just kept on going - slowly, slowly - until the darkness breathed out all over her in a great sigh, so cold that it seemed to freeze her right there where she was.

She tried to take another step, but couldn't. She could only stand shivering - and, with her voice shivering too, she asked, "What is it? Who are you?" For somehow, she knew that she was being watched, and disapproved of.

But all she could see for quite a while were the rocky walls of the cavern. Then, she thought she noticed a movement in part of those walls. The sort of movement that the shadow of a cloud makes as it passes over a valley. Only this movement settled and stayed, like a deep frown.

And now that she had seen it, she couldn't see anything else. It seemed to be everywhere. She felt that even the coldness of the air itself was puckering into a frown.

"Oh Wally," she whispered. "I don't like this!"

"You fidn't rissen, fid you?" he snapped. "Vit's *brad* deing nere."

"Why is it bad? I want to know!" Thel insisted.

"Zecause -" he answered, hopping around in front and butting his head against her, trying to push her back where she had come from - "zecause vit's a trave."

Thel looked puzzled. "A trave? Whatever do you mean by that, Wally? Let me see: wave - slave - knave - cave. Cave?" she asked, uncertainly.

Scowling, he repeated, "I trold you! Vit's a trave."

And suddenly she understood. "Well then, even if it *is* a grave, why can't I see it?"

"Zecause . . . !" And Wally thumped his tail on the ground, which was another way of stamping his foot.

This argument might have gone on for the next few thousand years, only that, right then, Thel heard something else - and somehow, she knew that it was the voice of the frown . . . a soft-around-the-edges kind of voice, yet threatening, too:

"Woe to those whose footsteps tread

Midst the spirits of the dead."

That made all the difference. Spirits of the dead? Ghosts? "Wally, let's go!" she murmured, urgently - and off she ran, with Wally springing after her, muttering goodness-knows-what under his breath.

In fact, she didn't stop running until she had turned eleven corners - and now, panting for breath in a large, empty cavern, she said to Wally, "I'm not scared of ghosts, but I don't like being shooed away, either."

Wally looked up at her sideways for a moment, then hopped around the entire cavern three times, chanting,

"Shooed or crabbed - bood or gad . . .

You can fee - rollow me!"

"No - no! I won't follow you !" she cried.
"I don't want to be shooed *or* grabbed."

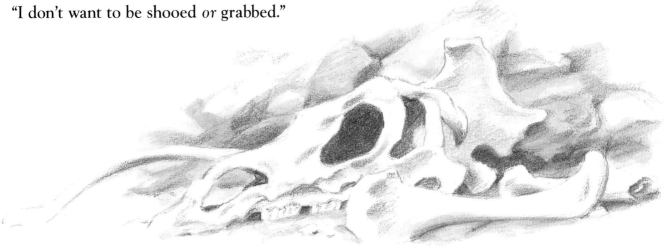

"Hoo late · hoo late . . ."
Wally's voice kept repeating,
growing fainter and fainter · as Thel
began to feel that, instead of standing upright,
she was sloping over, then air-tumbling · and this,
when she got used to it, was a very nice feeling indeed.

But all too soon, she came to an abrupt stop · hard up against a rocky wall,
with strange little whispery sounds going on around her. And right there in front
of her was an awful lot of water.

"Oh no!" she thought. "Not another pool to fall into!" And she pressed
herself even harder against the rocky wall, as she peered down into it.

But no, it wasn't a pool, because it was moving · slowly streaming.

"A sort of river, then? The Styx River, perhaps?" she asked herself. "Where
the Blue Lake comes from?"

Holding tightly on to a ledge of rock, she leaned forward and looked right
down into it · and there was the reflection of her own face looking straight
back at her.

But it didn't seem to be alone, down there. Or perhaps she was just imagining,
as her uncle would have said, because no sooner did she
think she saw something rippling playfully around
her reflection, than it slithered away
out of shape.

Then she thought she saw another - and another - with pinpoints of light that flashed on and off, like eyes blinking, and with long watery strands like hair, except that they never began or ended anywhere.

And it was from there that the strange little whispery sounds were coming.

"I wonder if they're saying anything?" Thel asked herself.

"Of course they're saying something," answered a deep, rumbling voice, from off in the distance somewhere. "Styxies are always saying something. They're saying what fun it is, having your reflection to play with - and please, could they keep it for always?"

"Oh!" Thel exclaimed, with a little gasp. And somehow couldn't think of anything else to say. Keep her reflection for always? "Oh my goodness!" she thought. "Then *I'd* have to stay here for always. I'd never see Elsie again. Or Uncle Peter. Or anyone."

"No, no," the mysterious, rumbling voice answered. "*You* can go whenever you like - as long as you leave your reflection with them."

No!" Thel cried out, suddenly realizing what Wally had meant about being grabbed rather than shooed. "I can't! I won't! It's my reflection - my very own!"

Hearing this, the whispery sounds that the styxies made became agitated and much louder.

"I thought so," rumbled the invisible voice. "They're most upset. They want a new sort of reflection to play with, after millions of years of only stalactites and things. Don't you think you could spare yours? Do you really have much use for it yourself?"

Thel hesitated. She couldn't think of anything particularly important that she ever used her reflection for, and yet -

"You see, it - it's the only one I've got," she explained, rather plaintively.

But that didn't sound like a good enough reason for not parting with it.

And the invisible voice didn't think so either: "Surely you don't actually need it, though!"

Meanwhile, down there in the river, the bright-eyed little styxies frolicked around with it happily, as though it were a bouncy toy.

"Oh dear - I don't know what to do," Thel muttered, thinking aloud. Then immediately - "Yes, I do know. I've *got* to keep it, otherwise I wouldn't be able to keep me, either."

"Really?

"Yes, really - truly! That's the way it *is* with reflections, and shadows, and things like that."

"Did you hear that, styxies?"

Whether they did or not, Thel was now very anxious to get herself and her reflection well away from here.

So, she hurried along the narrow pathway beside the river, at the same time keeping a very watchful eye on the styxies. And there they were, taking turns at holding on to both sides of her precious reflection, gliding and rippling forward with it, and making their soft whispery sounds in quite a friendly way, once more.

In fact, she was watching them so hard that she didn't realize how close she was to another great rocky wall - this one covered with beautiful fluted draperies - until she bumped into it.

"By Great Old Age, you don't look where you're going, do you?" said the same deep, rumbling voice that Thel had been hearing ever since she met the styxies. Now, though, it sounded close enough to be right above her. And sure enough - way up high, at the very top of her "wall", there were a lot of furrows and wrinkles which looked almost like a smile.

"Goodness!" Thel murmured, somehow reminded of Mr Tite, except that his face had been down instead of up. "Oh my goodness!"

And suddenly the furrows and wrinkles widened into a low, rumbling laugh. Without knowing it, Thel had bumped headlong into River Cave.

CHAPTER 6

Lucas Remembers

At the same moment, something came whizzing through the air making a little high-pitched squeal, before disappearing up into the roof somewhere.

"What was that ?" Thel asked herself. But before anyone could answer her, here it came again, whirring out of nowhere.

"Why, it's a bat!" she thought, putting her hands up over her head and crouching back against River Cave's draperies, for it seemed to be making straight towards her.

"That's no bat worthy of the name," grumbled the voice of River Cave. "That's young Scatty - the silliest creature that ever lived."

Whereupon Scatty Bat, with a joyful "Whee-ee-ee!" took a gliding leap up to where River Cave's face was, and flew around it six or seven times, cheekily brushing one of his wings against its rather haughty nose.

"Stop that, you impossible creature! Away with you! Go back to sleep!" River Cave shouted.

"If you say so," Scatty answered, with something between a squeak and a whistle - and immediately clutched at the top of River Cave's head with one of his little claws, then swung himself upside-down into his favourite resting position, with his wings folded down alongside of him, right over River Cave's face.

"Not there !" bellowed River Cave, with such a blast that Scatty shot straight up and collided with one of the stalactites on the roof, then came

gzagging down again, bumping into things everywhere, like a frisky pony in a
ɔom full of furniture, and finally landed flat on his back over a little white hump
n the ground, with an extremely foolish grin on his face.

Thel burst out laughing. And suddenly, there was Wally, hopping around in
circles, as though he were laughing too.

But River Cave himself was not laughing. "Look at you!" he cried out.
"Carbonated calcium, just *look* at you - draped over my youngest stalagmite - "

"Stalag what?" Thel interrupted.

"Mite!" snapped River Cave. "First a stalactite, then a stalagmite. That's
the way the water drips."

"Oh," said Thel, as though that explained everything.

"Only about two and a half thousand years old, no more. Has the makings in
her of another Minaret - "

That had a familiar sound to Thel, then she remembered one of the picture
postcards of special cave things that her cousin had been buying to send to people.

"Yes, another Minaret. Then an illiterate young bat comes along - "

"Illiterate?" Thel interrupted again.

"Yes, yes! Can't even read his own echoes - the first thing that any self-
respecting bat learns - doesn't know where he's going or why - and ends up there -
right there - just look at him! - catching every waterdrop he can - stunting the
growth of my littlest, most precious stalagmite!"

And indeed there he was, the naughty thing, lying with his eyes closed and
his mouth open, with a steady procession of waterdrops splashing straight into it
from a stalactite up on the roof.

Wally hopped round in a few more circles of sheer glee.

"And not just waterdrops, either," River Cave added, dolefully, "but
lime-carriers, builders, sculptors, cave-makers - "

"Cave-makers?" Thel repeated. "Just all on their own, with no one to
help them?"

"No, no, no, child - of course not! With the Wizard to help them."

"The Wizard?"

"Of course the Wizard. Everybody knows that. The Wizard Great Old Age."

"Is he around here anywhere? Could I meet him?" asked Thel.

But if River Cave answered her, she didn't hear him, because, at that very moment, a loud noise thundered out, somewhere in the distance. Loud enough, surely, to be echoing into every cavern and crevice in this whole underground world. And not only echoing, but making everything shake, as well - even the ground.

Thel toppled off balance, and noticed Wally leaping over toward the towering figure of River Cave. So she hurried after him and, together, they crept round behind him.

Thel's heartbeats were racing, and Wally's little front feet were quivering.

Then, with a deep rumble of laughter, River Cave said, "Upon my lime, he's at it again, the foolish fellow!"

Whatever it was that *who* ever was up to again, Thel didn't think it was anything to laugh at - and Wally's little front feet kept quivering as hard as ever. But when River Cave went on chuckling away to himself, Thel did at last peep around and ask, "Who's up to what, Mr River Cave?"

"Old Lucas, of course. Remembering. Even after millions of years, he still can't forget. Then he sees to it that nobody else can forget, either."

The thundering noises now became quite deafening, and seemed to be right on top of them. Then, a huge boulder came smashing down like a landslide, and trembled to a standstill only a few inches away from them.

With a gasp, Thel darted out of sight again, behind River Cave.

"Come, come, you two!" he said.

"Remember, it's only a memory. All of this happened a long, long time ago. If only old Lucas wouldn't keep stirring it up again!"

But apparently, now that he had started, Lucas had no intention of stopping. And as he went on brooding about the fearsome earthquakes which had happened to him millions of years ago, he made them all as real again now as they had been then.

Rocks and boulders kept crashing around everywhere, as though some invisible giant were picking them up and hurling them down at random. Then, Wally and Thel felt the ground itself lifting, rolling, slithering - and carrying them away with it.

"Oh Wally, where are we going?" she asked. "Where's River Cave? And little Scatty? What's happened to Scatty?"

But then, there was a sudden deafening sound of cracking or splintering. Wally jumped with fright, Thel looked up just in time to see a beautiful white column breaking in two - and a loud grating voice rang out through the huge cavern of fallen rocks which had opened up around them -

"My column! By beautiful column! Wrecked! Ruined! For ever!" - followed by a great sob, like thunder rumbling, then total silence and stillness, with not a single thing moving.

Even Thel and Wally stayed perfectly still, clinging to each other. And Thel had the strongest feeling that she had seen this column already - broken, as it was now. Then she remembered another of Elsie's picture postcards, and - "Of course!" she murmured. "The Broken Column!"

"Why, Mr Lucas Cave - wherever you are - " she called out, not the least bit afraid now, "you shouldn't feel so bad about it. Your Broken Column is one of the very special things about Jenolan. Everybody wants to come and see it."

But nobody answered her.

"Oh dear! I do wish I could see you, Mr Lucas!"

Then, turning and gazing all around her, she realized that everything was different again. Somehow, the Broken Column had disappeared, and something - she didn't quite know what - made her feel that she was in a church with a great high ceiling, and with an organ playing.

But the "organ" turned out to be a voice. And when she looked to see where it came from, there - way up high near the top of this new, vast cavern - the rocky wall looked so much like a face that she asked, rather timidly, "Are - are *you* Mr Lucas?"

"Who else would I be?" the organ voice swelled out once more - at the same moment as a host of other voices sounded, and the shuffle of many footsteps.

Then, the light in the great cavern changed. Instead of being the warm sort of glow that seemed to radiate out from deep inside the rocky walls of this whole magical cave world, it became sharper, and it lit up only one part at a time. "That's human light," Thel told herself. And indeed, here came another group of cave visitors, with a guide in their midst.

"Hullo, everyone!" she shouted, this time thinking what a joke it was that nobody could see or hear her.

Neither did they see a sudden swift movement, as Scatty Bat came flying, high up, into this huge cavern, like a little black shadow.

He crashed one of his wings against the wall, just a scratch away from Lucas's frowning face, then shot straight down to where the visitors were.

"Whee-ee-ee!" he whistled shrilly. And if he was supposed to be guiding himself by the echoes from that whistle, it didn't work like that, for the next moment he was fluttering and tangling amongst all of the people, with nobody knowing a single thing about it - just gazing and marvelling at everything around them.

At last, their guide said, "So there you have it - the great Cathedral Cavern. And the acoustics here are quite remarkable. See for yourselves! Has anyone got a singing voice? If so, don't be shy - give us a song!

Almost immediately, one of the women did start singing, in a clear, high voice. And Thel, scarcely daring to breathe, watched with wonder as little wisps of colour floated up into the air, then went dancing and frolicking around - more and more of them, sprays and fountains and showers of them - until the whole cavern seemed to be filled with rainbow fairies.

As soon as the singing stopped, everyone clapped, and started talking at once, having no idea that a million scraps of rainbow were fading into soft little colour echoes, before disappearing altogether.

Nor did they see the antics of Scatty, as he chased around trying in vain to catch them. He whizzed up to a yellow one, only to have it mischievously tweek at his ears, then vanish.

He did a crazy back-flip after a blue one, which went sailing through the air a whisper in front of him until he bumped his nose against a stalagmite.

A white one, catching at his claws, swung herself out and away into space like a little trapeze flier.

Finally, he plunged headlong into a group of purple and orange ones, which mercilessly tickled his wings, sending him off into a tumbling, spinning roll of giggles.

And that was exactly what Thel and Wally felt like doing.

It was only after Scatty himself had gone flying away to sleep it off somewhere that Thel, thinking back, said quietly, "You know, Wally I think it's even nicer seeing a song than hearing it."

CHAPTER 7
The Crystal City

Wally didn't say anything about that. He'd already forgotten the song fairies. He looked like somebody listening with his eyes and thinking with his ears.

"Curds and boblins!" he muttered.

"What was that?" Thel asked.

"Pegs and queds," he answered.

"Really, Wally, these words of yours! I don't suppose you mean anything so easy as Ps and Qs, do you?"

But all he did was to spring off his tail and out of sight, in one great bound - just as Thel heard a rushing of wings and footsteps right behind her.

She made a dash after Wally, but instead, found herself being knocked off balance and jostled along willynilly amidst a huge crowd of the oddest things she had ever seen.

There was a pair of giraffe legs with nothing on top of them . . . and an elephant's head with nothing below it - just floating through the air, coiling its trunk around and smiling pleasantly. There was a beautiful white veil with sparkles all over it, gliding along gracefully with no one inside it.

There were flocks of geese with bright-orange beaks, flying above everything else in straight white lines.

And there were hosts of extraordinary little creatures rather like large insects with impossible shapes. Some had antlers instead of heads, or corkscrews instead of arms, others had three or four legs instead of two, or bodies like the letter O. And all of them kept leaping, spinning and cartwheeling around like goblin acrobats.

"Goblins!" Thel repeated silently. "Could these be Wally's 'boblins'? They must be, I suppose. And the geese - the birds - would be his 'curds'. But what about the 'pegs' and 'queds'? Yes of course - legs and heads."

And she was having such fun working out the riddles of Wally's language that she forgot about wondering whether or not all of these strange beings were friendly, or about where they might be going in such a hurry, carrying her along with them. Then, above all of the flapping wings and scraping footsteps, she heard a familiar, piercing sound - and there, way up near the roof, was Scatty.

"Whee-ee-ee!" he whistled, darting down towards them, but quickly forgot where he was going, and went shooting off in a different direction.

"Whee-ee-ee!" he shrilled again - and this time came tumbling through space like a reel of something unrolling, finally landing face-down and with wings wide-spread, right on top of the giraffe legs.

But nobody seemed to notice this, any more than they were noticing Thel. So Scatty just went bobbing along up there, looking very pleased with himself on a fine new pair of legs.

Thel wanted to laugh, but felt rather scared of attracting any attention, amongst all of these weird creatures.

Then the elephant's head, still smiling, stretched out its trunk and delicately lifted the little bat up into the air. Scatty wriggled and squealed, but the elephant merely twirled him around a few times, before tossing him up high and catching him, like a ball.

Scatty squealed again, protesting loudly - and at that same moment, everybody came to an abrupt stop.

Scatty gave one of the elephant's ears a sharp little bite, then flew off to hang upside-down on the first rocky ledge he could bump into.

But Thel was anxious to know why everyone had stopped so suddenly, and craned her head around trying to find out. All she could see were the folds of a beautiful canopy, sparkling with whiteness. But it must have been draped over the couch of somebody very important, for now, as the creatures all stood facing it, one of them wailed, "Your jewels, oh Imperial one! Your precious jewels!"

"Broken into - scattered - " a second one crackled out.

"Lost!" moaned a third.

"Stolen!" shouted a fourth.

And a murmur of indignation rippled amongst them all, just as one of the geese, arriving late, collided with Thel instead of landing properly, and sent her sprawling on to the ground with a startled cry.

Immediately, all of the creatures turned and looked at her, seeing her for the first time.

"That's who it is!" squealed one of the goblins - or heligoblins, as the cave people called them - whose hair twisted out around his head in masses of knots, loops and spirals. And, with a babble of angry voices, the whole lot of them together made a rush and a grab for her, so that she could quite easily have been squashed out of existence.

37

But instead, part of the glistening canopy quickly floated across and wrapped itself around her. And a strong yet gentle pressure came down on the top of her head, which rather made her feel as if she was going down in a very fast lift. Then something else, like a giant hand, slowly picked her up, and set her down again in what looked like a sort of Fairyland.

It was a whole city of houses and towers, fir-trees and spires, all made of crystal.

There was even a soft sparkle in the air, like crystals shimmering.

And a great wall surrounded it, pleating in and out, and going way off into the distance, much farther than she could see.

Thel had no idea of where she was, or of who had put her there, but it was certainly the prettiest place she had ever seen.   And - best of all -she felt perfectly safe there.

"No one would ever think of looking for me here," she told herself.

Then she realized that there was nobody around anyway. Not even Wally. And she was beginning to wonder if she really liked the idea of having a whole city to herself - even a magical one like this - when she heard something like a bell ringing, or cymbals chiming - but ringing or chiming in actual words:

"You silly little scatter-limes! Surely you've been here long enough to know that I've never been able to keep my jewels hidden away tidily in a box. They're always just lying around."

A soft, apologetic sort of murmur, in many voices, seemed to answer.

"Yet all of a sudden," the chimes went on, "you get all worked up about thieves and vandals."

Another chorus of shame-faced murmuring.

"Then to make things worse, a mortal child comes visiting us. A very special mortal child, who has somehow slipped through into our 'other-world' of magic. And you nearly frighten nine stalactites out of her! Whatever would Great Old Age, our Wizard, have to say about you?"

The murmuring of apology was now scarcely louder than a whisper.

"If it weren't for him, none of you would even *be* here. And haven't you learnt anything in all the time he's given you?"

Thel stood listening to this with more and more wonder.

"So that," she thought, "must be the one who rescued me, and put me here. What a giant she must be! Perhaps one of the Caves themselves."

Suddenly a huge furry thing came bounding at a great pace, right over her and the whole of her crystal city.

"Oh my goodness! Another giant!" And when she stood up on tiptoe to watch it going off into the distance, she realized that it was a wallaby. "A giant wallaby!" her thinking said.

"In fact, *your* wallaby," the beautiful chiming voice of Imperial Cave rang out, this time with laughter in it.

"And what's more, time to get things back to normal."

Once again, Thel could feel something pressing down on the top of her head, only this time it was as though she were in a very fast lift going up.

With amazement, she watched as the crystal city and its miles of "fortifications" fell away from her, growing smaller and smaller every second. And there she was, face-to-face with a beautiful "bride"- looking lady, all white and sparkly, wearing a pure-white veil over her head and around her shoulders, glistening with jewels.

"Did you make me little enough to hide in that tiny city down there?" Thel asked. "And then big enough to be me again?"

Imperial's laughter was a soft ringing of bells.

"But - you're not a giant after all, then. And - you only pressed the top of my head. The same both times."

"Ah, but the first time, I used my right hand, and the second time my left one."

"Oh I see," said Thel, not feeling at all sure that she did.

"Haven't you heard of Right and Left Imperial?"

Thel shook her head. "No. Just Imperial, I'm afraid."

"Yes, yes, I'd forgotten - they've changed it." And the musical chiming of the Cave's voice sounded quite forlorn. "What a pity! Because there's such a difference between right and left." Then suddenly, she was all happiness and sparkle again. "Off you go, now, young Thel, and find out for yourself."

"How? Where?" Thel asked.

"You'll see," chimed Imperial.
Or at least, that was what Thel imagined she said, because all at once the ringing voice sounded only faintly, like an echo - and the only thing left of Imperial herself was a beautiful glistening white veil draped over a large rock.

CHAPTER 8
"Going Nowhere In Particular"

Thel took one more fond look at the lovely little crystal city with its fortifications, then thought about Wally again - that monster who had gone thumping past while she herself was the size of a bird-seed - and wondered where he might have got to now.

She also thought about Great Old Age, remembering what Imperial Cave had told her family of "scatter-limes" about him, and wondering if she herself would ever meet him.

"He certainly *must* be a wizard, if none of these caves could ever have happened without him. And yet . . . Great - Old - Age!" She repeated his name slowly, pondering its meaning. "If he isn't a 'person' kind of wizard, but - well, time that goes on for ever, *could* I meet him? Could *anybody* meet him?"

Still asking herself questions that she couldn't answer, and wondering what could possibly happen next, Thel went strolling off along a narrow passageway and down a few steps - "going nowhere in particular," she supposed.

The very moment she thought this, however, strange things began to happen. First, she couldn't feel what she was walking on.

Then, she fell straight down on to her back a tiny distance above the ground. Next, the strip of air she was lying on started moving, carrying her backwards - slowly to begin with, then faster and faster, until everything was a big grey blur.

She began to wonder if she might have stumbled into a wind tunnel - but went speeding past the idea before she could finish it.

She couldn't even finish the feeling of being scared before she had passed this, too, by another million years. For it wasn't space that Thel was zipping through, but time. Hundreds of millions of years of it. Back to when the Earth itself was young . . .

Until there she was at last, quite sure that she must be dreaming, for she was breathing and gliding about happily at the bottom of the sea, in an enchanted garden of shells and corals, just as though that were a perfectly natural thing to do.

Then she turned a corner - and it must have been a corner in time, because suddenly everything was changed, with hundreds of little fish-like creatures darting around her and amidst the corals in all directions, very busy with whatever keeps fish-like creatures busy.

"This is the most magic place I've ever been to in my whole life," she thought, with a deep sigh of wonder. "Oh, if only Elsie could see it! When I wake up, I'll tell her all about it. But no, I couldn't - not even if I kept talking for the rest of my life." Off she went with her new little fish-like friends, flitting around for what felt like hours.

"I could do this for ever and ever," she thought.

But as happens so often, just as everything seems tidily arranged, something comes along to throw it all into confusion - and now, for Thel, that "Something" made her suddenly go stiff

with panic, for when she turned her head, casually looking around, she found herself face to face with the biggest, longest animal she had ever seen. There it was speeding straight towards her with its head thrown back and its mouth open full of dagger like teeth - while she, stunned with terror, couldn't seem to move, or even to think.

Then, just as the monster was about to snap its jaws shut around her, it seemed as if a great suction pulled her down into even greater depths of this dark-blue ocean, leaving the monster guessing, and having to satisfy itself by gulping a few hundred sort-of fish instead.

"Oh thank you - thank you!" Thel murmured, not knowing who or what had rescued her, and unable to see anything except darkness. And there she stayed for quite a long time - until at last, very timidly, she let herself float up out of this underwater "canyon", to where she had been before, amongst corals and sea-lilies and pretty little fish-like creatures.

But she still didn't feel carefree, as she had been before the monster, so she quickly made over towards a grotto where she might be able to hide. And there, just inside it, was another creature different from anything she had ever seen.

It looked as if it had a coat of plated armour, and it was pushing itself along the ground with crab-like legs

- or were they fins? And, queerest of all, its two eyes were perched up on the top of its head.

It didn't look actually frightening, like the monster, but Thel felt frightened anyway, and backed off as quickly as she could. Which wasn't very quick at all, because of the throngs of fish - or sort of fish - now jostling around her in such swarms that she almost had to push her way amongst them, waving them aside with one hand after the other.

It was only after she had been doing this for quite a while that she realized that, instead of fish crowding around her, they were people just like herself - and that, instead of being under water, they were under ground, gazing and marvelling at the rocky walls towering up around them, while her special friend the White Star Man explained how, millions of years ago, all of this used to be the ocean floor.

"Look carefully," he said, "and you'll see that the walls are filled with fossils - mostly of coral, because right here where we're standing would have been part of a vast coral reef."

"Yes, that's right!" Thel called out excitedly. "I know, because I've been there. Right now! I've just come back this very minute - from the bottom of the sea!"

"What was that?" asked the White Star Man, glancing at the people nearest him. But nobody answered.

"I thought somebody said something."

"Yes, I did!" said Thel.

But he didn't hear that, and just went on talking about this part of the caves, which used to be called the Left Imperial.

"I know - I know! Imperial Cave told me!" Thel shouted, even though she knew that nobody could hear her.

"Looks like cauliflowers," said one of the visitors, pointing to a part of the walls around this passageway. "And not very fresh ones, at that."

Everyone smiled, and their guide answered, "You're right. You'll notice that a fair bit of this cave looks quite grubby. That's because it's been more exposed than the others - to weather, and even to red dust-storms. And the cauliflower look has probably been caused by air-currents, disturbing the natural movement of waterdrops."

Which was all very well, but Thel was far too excited to stand around listening any longer. After all, when you've spent the last few minutes travelling backwards and forwards in time, and darting about amongst coral reefs at the bottom of ancient seas, it's hard to stay still in the one spot while somebody gives a lesson - even if that somebody is the White Star Man.

So Thel went skipping off down a wide pathway between great rocky walls filled with fossils that were millions of years old. And she wasn't the least bit worried about not knowing where she was going or what might happen next.

What did happen next was that she heard a quiet little "thud - thud - thud" following along behind her. She turned to see - and there was Wally, all soft and brown, with mischief in his eyes.

"Oh Wally!" Thel exclaimed, kneeling down, putting her arms around him, and nestling her face into the warm furriness of his coat. "You can't imagine where I've been - and you wouldn't believe me if I told you."

But Wally, with a wriggle and a hop, jumped on to a rock shelf and, looking down at her, excitedly gabbled an awful lot of stuff that Thel sort of understood without decoding any of the words separately . . .

"Olly snows efling - es - es - es! All aflong, Olly snows efling! Olly finks it, and flans it, and yawks to the Blizzard, and flakes it all yappen - es - es - es!"

"Oh really!" Thel exclaimed, laughing. "So you know about it all, do you, Wally? And you even talk to the Wizard about it, then make it all happen. Well, I don't know whether to believe you or not. You're a bit of a rascal - and boastful, too."

Cocking his head sideways, Wally seemed to like the sound of that very much indeed.

"Anyway, I'm going," said Thel - and off she went again, running around what felt rather like the bottom of a canyon.

Wally jumped down and followed her, but only for a minute. He was a leader, not a follower. So, with a great leap off his tail, he swept past her.

Thel ran to keep up with him, watching where she was putting her feet rather than anything else - until suddenly, it was as though a huge spider sprang out at her from a high crevice, all white and gleaming, with a thousand glittering eyes, and twice as many legs coiling, twisting, and reaching out to grab her. Quite different from the shy, gentle little spiders in the Grand Arch.

Thel screamed, and jumped backwards - as it happened, right up against the White Star Man, who had walked a little ahead of his group of visitors to throw the next light switch.

"Oh!" Thel cried out. "Oh thank you, Mr Star Man!" - creeping behind him, and feeling quite safe there in fact, brave enough to peep around and stare that terrible spider in the eye - or rather, in all of its eyes.

But evidently the mortal visitors didn't see it like that, because when the Star Man shone a special light on to it, they all gasped with wonder. "It's the most glorious thing I've ever seen!" one of them said.

"Right," the Star Man agreed. "And it's called the Mystery. Does anyone know why?"

The visitors shuffled around a bit - on their feet and in their minds - but no one made any suggestions.

"Well, simply because it *is* a mystery," their guide told them. "Remember - just the same as stalactites, stalagmites, shawls, and so on, this has been formed by water, seeping through from the outside world, drop by drop, ever so slowly, for thousands of years. And it's easy to understand water dripping downwards. But look at all these shapes - by the way, we call them helictites - branching out sideways, curling around in circles, going upwards, in spirals, in every direction imaginable. And how can you explain the slow, slow dripping of water doing that ?"

Thel could almost hear everybody thinking around in circles, and in every other way that her fearsome "spider" was twisting its countless legs. Then one of them suggested, "Air currents?"

"No, not in this part of the cave."

After a moment's silence, somebody else said, "Gravity gone mad?" And everyone laughed.

"Of course, scientific knowledge is very important. But in this case - well, these little fellows have kept their secret for so long that, in a way, I wish they could keep it for ever." And everyone smiled.

Soon, the group moved off to be shown more of this cave, which Thel kept thinking of as the left side of Imperial.

And she followed along with them for a while, until they were well away from the twisting arms and legs of the giant white "spider".

"Helictites", the Star Man called them. She supposed that was the human name for heligoblins - and she wanted to get as far away from them as possible.

"You do, do you?" asked a low, rumbling voice which sounded as if it had travelled great distances through a rocky tunnel, and was still a long way off somewhere.

Wally stood listening, turning his head and his ears in every direction. And Thel gazed around everywhere too, seeing nothing that looked even slightly as if it might have spoken.

"Well, this is a mighty improbable place to have come to if you don't like heligobs," the mysterious voice added.

Taking a few steps on tiptoe and resting a hand on Wally's head, Thel whispered, "Do you know who it is, Wally?"

Then, bravely, she went and stood where she could see every corner of this great cavern, and where every corner of it could see *her*.

"Are you - please tell me, are you the Wizard?" she asked, very respectfully. "The - the Wizard Great Old Age?"

The answer to this was a bellowing laugh, again with that tunnelly sort of sound, and loud enough to fill the whole cavern. But the next moment, it was muffled out by an even louder noise, right beside her, and rather like the whirring of giant wings.

Then suddenly, she was sailing way up high, above everything - and she realized with amazement that there was a huge, feathery white wing moving gently up and down on one side of her, and a huge feathery reddish-gold one moving up and down, just as gently, on her other side.

CHAPTER 9
"No Other Possible Explanation"

Scary things had happened to her so many times since that long-ago morning when she had followed Wally into the wizardry of Jenolan, that Thel was almost used to them by now. And she realized that, no matter how terrifying they might have seemed to begin with, she had never been actually hurt by any of them.

So now, she was happily enjoying this new adventure of flying through the air on somebody else's wings when, without any warning, she was set down again. Not on the ground, however, but in a very dangerous position indeed - on a tiny platform at the top of a great tall pillar, with no rails to hold on to.

This, apart from the prehistoric sea monster, was the worst thing that had ever happened to her. She knew it was. She was far too scared to look down, and almost too scared to breathe. And something made her feel that she couldn't - mustn't - call out to anyone.

Again as though bellowing through a long tunnel, an invisible somebody - perhaps the owner of the wings - boomed out, "There you are, Orient. I've brought you a present."

"What present?" asked a voice with a sort of echo and a smile in it.

"A statue for your Pillar of Hercules. What else?"

"But - "

"I know, I know - it isn't a Hercules. There weren't any available. But it is, at least, a Thel."

By the sound of her voice, Orient wasn't the least bit pleased.

"Take her down from there at once, Baal! You ought to be ashamed of yourself, playing tricks like that. And using angels' wings for the purpose, too. Angels, indeed!"

"What's wrong with that?"

"If people knew the truth about you, angels would be the farthest things from their minds."

"Oh please!" Thel whisper-murmured, not daring to open her mouth wide enough to call out, in case she toppled off her tiny perch in the process.

It really did seem as if these two - Baal and Orient Caves - might argue so much that they'd forget all about her. But now, with her soft little "Oh please!" echoing around the huge cavern until it sounded as if she was saying it about five times instead of once, Orient's own echoing voice commanded sternly:

"Baal, get her down from there this very century, otherwise I'll set your heligoblins on to you."

"Threats - threats!" Baal grumbled, from the depths of the red tunnel that humans called his Dragon's Throat. "Who's afraid of heligobs, anyway?"

Now this was the worst thing that Baal could have said, because there were more heligoblins in his cave than in any others - striding around boldly out in the open, or hiding away in ambush, and always crowding into spaces big enough for only half their number. And there is scarcely anything anywhere more mischievous than a heligoblin.

So now, feeling encouraged by Orient and insulted by Baal, a great swarm of them rushed in together to show Baal that if he wasn't afraid of them, he should be.

Some of them tugged feathers out of his wings, then mixed them up into a hopeless muddle, sticking white feathers into his reddish-gold wing, and reddish-gold feathers into his white one.

About twenty of them went somersaulting down his Dragon's Throat, which felt like swallowing flies.

They swung from his ear-lobes, and jabbed at him with crystal splinters.

They tore strips off his robe - the famous Cloth of Gold - and tied his ankles together with them. And they all kept yelling out war-cries in their high, thin voices - especially when Baal started bellowing at them.

And Orient had never had more fun in her life.

So much so that she did indeed forget about Thel until, rolling her eyes up in glee, she happened to catch sight of the little "statue" trembling on top of her great pillar, and shouted above the racket of the heligoblins,

"Baal, *do* something! You put her there - now take her down again! Suppose I got myself a heap of bones, like some of the other caves - can you imagine the trouble I'd be in?"

Baal rumbled out a dragon-throaty sort of laugh.

"Be serious for once! Don't you know that I'd be accused of - what's the word? It's an 'ism' beginning with 'play'."

Because Thel had always been good at words, "plagiarism" popped into her mind - then quickly popped out of it again, before she could lose her balance by saying it aloud.

But Orient heard her thought, anyway, and was delighted with it. "That's *it*, you clever child! Get her down from there, Baal! Can't you see how useful she could be?"

But Baal was still tangled up in his Cloth of Gold. As soon as he wriggled his ankles free, the heligoblins sprang in and knotted up his wrists.

Meanwhile, Wally had been anxiously watching Thel from down on the ground somewhere. Certainly he hadn't planned for anything like this to happen. And Scatty had been watching her just as anxiously from somewhere in the roof.

"Perhaps I could rescue her," he heard himself say with one of his wide-awake ears.

"Then I'd be a hero, wouldn't I?" he heard with his other ear.

"There'd be songs written about me," he heard with both of them together.

So - without stopping to work out the meaning of echo messages, as any well-read bat would have done - he just came rushing across and crashed straight into Thel, knocking her headlong off the Pillar of Hercules.

Down she went with a terrified scream, falling through space - and this time, without any wings.

Whistle-squeaking with alarm, Scatty flew round and round in useless circles. And Wally, from down below, looked on with staring eyes and quivering paws.

Then, all in a moment, Thel realized that she was no longer falling, but gliding - and that, although there were still no wings about her, something else *was*. Something rippling with colour, that she was actually sitting on, just like a magic carpet.

Without daring to move or to ask herself any questions, she began to catch glimpses of wonderful columns, theatres, statues, draperies, bridges and temples, in one after another of Orient's great palaces, as she rode above and amongst them.

Everywhere there were shawls and draperies of glowing reds, golds and frosty white, some like dainty fringes, others hanging immensely from great heights. And now that she realized it, Thel's own magic carpet was one of these.

"I must be dreaming - I *must* be!" she told herself. "Nobody rides on magic carpets these days."

"Really? Don't they?" asked the smiling voice that Thel recognized as Orient's. "Perhaps you have to be a Thel to ride on one. Yes - yes - there's no other possible explanation."

Thel looked around everywhere, trying to find a face to go with the voice. It sounded as if it was right beside her; yet, just as easily, it could have been coming from miles away.

But way up near the roof, and unaware of all this, Scatty was still squealing around in wild circles of bat-panic.

"Scatty, it's all right!" Thel called out to him. "Stop worrying! Look - here I am - on a magic carpet!"

"Eek!" he shrilled, unable to think of anything else to say.

"That's right. And all because of you. If it weren't for you, this might never have happened."

Scatty suddenly stopped whirling, and hovered for a moment in the one spot, peering down at Thel.

Then - in a voice that sounded like a pair of scissors running through silk - he cried out, "Scatty's a hero?"

"He certainly is."

"There's a song about Scatty?"

"There will be," Thel promised him. "I'll see to it myself. Listen - here it comes. This is the chorus. I'll write the verses later -

'Through Legend, History, and all of that, There's none so daring as Scatty Bat.' "

Scatty listened to this, and was so excited about it that he plummeted down and grabbed at one corner of the floating carpet, which would have tip-tilted it into a roller-coaster if it *hadn't* been magic.

Then - as it still kept sailing around peacefully among Orient's palaces and cities - he dropped himself down from it like a swinging tassle, shrilling out again and again, "None so daring as Scatty Bat . . . None so daring . . . daring . . . daring . . . "

It was quite a few moments before Thel realized that his voice had been gradually fading off into the distance - and that she herself was no longer up in the air, but down on the ground again, in a kind of forest, all glistening white.

"Oh my goodness - where am I now ?" she asked herself. "And how did I get here, without landing or anything?"

Nobody answered her. But as she stood wondering what to do next, she heard a soft little sound from somewhere inside the forest - and suddenly, there was Wally.

She was delighted to see him, but had no intention of telling him so straight away.

"Now look here, Wally!" she said, sternly. "If it was also your idea, having me kidnapped, and left stranded on that awful Pillar of Hercules - "

He pricked one ear towards her, then the other - which could have meant anything or nothing.

Silently, he took a gentle, gliding hop away from her, back into the snow-white forest of stalactites and stalagmites that he had come from, then stopped and looked round, as though beckoning her to follow him, just as he had at the very beginning, out in the Grand Arch.

And because she was somehow reminded of this, she said softly, "Oh Wally, I've got a feeling - a very strange feeling . . . " But she didn't finish what she was thinking, because saying things sometimes makes realities of them, and she couldn't bear to imagine all of this magic coming to an end.

So, very quietly, she followed where he was leading her - into a silent world of sparkling whiteness, tinted here and there with a golden rosiness, like sunrise over snow. And it felt to her like the quietest place she had ever known, where the only tiny sounds were those of constantly falling waterdrops. Elfin music.

Something about it reminded her of what she had heard the Star Man saying once, about the wettest of the caves being the most "alive" ones - those that were growing the fastest. "So this one, whatever it is, must be growing at a blinding rate - perhaps an inch in a thousand years," she thought, not minding in the least that she was getting dripped on almost as much as if she were walking in misty rain.

On and on she went, with Wally just a little ahead of her - down long flights of steps, then up again, and around narrow little paths that twisted themselves into riddles of golden, rosy whiteness.

Frosty-looking spires massed up from the ground to meet tier upon tier of delicate fringes pouring down from the roof, and there were richly hanging curtains, ropes and tassles everywhere.

"It's all so beautiful, that I think I'll stay here for ever." She said this aloud, much to Wally's exasperation, judging by the way he stood glaring at her, with a thump of the tail and a toss of the head.

"No use going on like that, Wally. I'm puffed out and tired, and I think I'll have a little sleep."

Wally couldn't believe his ears. He jumped up and down several times, and made quick circles in the air with his tiny front feet. But all to no avail, for Thel simply couldn't keep her eyes open. Nor could she stop herself from slipping down on to the ground of what was actually Jubilee Cave, wet and all as it was.

CHAPTER 10
The Wizard

The White Star Man was just on his way back to the staff quarters after seeing a group of people through the fossils-and-Mystery cave, when he noticed Thel leaning against the stone wall overlooking the Blue Lake, and walked across to her instead.

"Good gracious - where have you been, young Thel, getting your clothes all wet like that?"

Thel turned and looked up at him doubtfully, as though wondering how it was that now, suddenly, he could see her. "Yes, I know," she answered, dreamily. "I couldn't help it - going off to sleep, I mean. And I remember - the ground was all wet."

"But - where?" he asked. And there was just something about the tone of his voice, and the way he looked at her, that made her say, scarcely above a whisper, "I never met the Wizard, though."

"You mean - Great Old Age?" he asked smiling.

She nodded.

"Well, that depends on how you expect to meet him. Actually, you *feel* him rather anything else. Very strongly indeed around Jenolan."

And Thel remembered the mysterious Something she had felt in her room that night, back in Caves House, understanding now what it must have been.

"But if you want to see him . . . " The Star Man hesitated, and turned to look across the road into the rugged, towering cavern called the Devil's Coach House.

Thel also turned and looked into it. "You mean - *that's* Great Old Age?" she asked.

"Of course. And what about all of this?" - waving his arm out toward the Grand Arch and everything around it. "To say nothing of the caves themselves - and in fact, the whole of this great, ancient continent."

"Oh my goodness!" Thel breathed, feeling quite overawed.

"But of course, you also see him in the colour of flowers, and in the light of every dawn, just as you can hear him in crashing waterfalls, and in the singing and chattering of birds."

Thel pondered this for a moment, then said with a little laugh, "I bet Billy the Bird Woman knows all about that."

"Indeed she does," the Star Man agreed, also laughing. "She more than most people." Then, turning serious again, "Off you go now, young lady, and change those wet clothes! Your cousin was looking everywhere for you. Said she hadn't seen you since breakfast."

"Oh - Elsie! For a moment, I - Oh dear me! *What* breakfast? How - how ever long ago?" Thel stammered.

"Why, today's breakfast, lassie - about two and a half hours ago."

Thel gazed at him, utterly bewildered.

The White Star Man nodded, smiling, almost as if he half knew something that he wasn't telling. And for a couple of seconds, it seemed as if the little stars clinging on to his lapels actually twinkled at her . . .

Thel was running through the Grand Arch toward Caves House, when she noticed a furry little brown wallaby standing up on top of a large rock, watching her.

"Wally!" she called out. "Oh Wally - Wally!"

But he looked as if he didn't know what she was talking about, and went bounding off among masses of boulders. Nothing could have told her more clearly that this, here, was the human world again - not any longer the magic one. So, rather sadly, she continued on along the wide roadway, walking now instead of running.

Just ahead of her, two women were also walking, and Thel heard one of them say, "There's that odd little creature again."

"H'm!" the other huffed indignantly. "Too odd for my liking, if you know what I mean."

Thel looked up over the embankment opposite Caves House, to see whom they were talking about. It was still covered with golden daisies - and perched in there amongst them, with a rosella on her shoulder, was Billy the Bird Woman.

Smiling her brightest smile, Thel stopped and waved to her - and Billy the Bird Woman waved back, to the tinkling of her twenty-seven bangles. Then, rippling with fun, she ruffled herself up as though into a flurry of feathers - and suddenly, over the embankment, there was nothing to be seen except a showering of yellow daisies, with gusty little breezes nodding their heads together.

AFTERWORD

The magic of Jenolan began way back among the mysteries of geological time. But for me, it began only about fifty years ago, when I first visited there. And everything about it - from the walnut-tree in front of Caves House to the hill covered with yellow daisies opposite, to the ducks and swans on its Blue Lake, to its thousands of wallabies and the grandeur of its arches and underground limestone palaces - was purest magic.

Today, while much of it remains the same, much of it is also different. The wonderful old walnut-tree, for instance, was struck by lightning some years ago, and that was the end of it - except for the fact that some of its timber was fashioned into the front part of the reception desk in Caves House. So it still, in a sense, lives on in Jenolan.

There's far fewer rock wallabies around at Jenolan these days but you might just spot one (perhaps it might be one of Wally's family) and you've got to be lucky to hear or see a sooty owl or to have a possum sneak into your room at Caves House.

And the special little spiders that build webs among the rocks in the Grand Arch are struggling to cope with all the fumes from motor traffic that goes through there everyday.

But now that we're beginning to recognize these problems we are also trying to rectify them. And that, largely, is what the Jenolan Caves Trust is all about.

I wonder if the time might come when furry little wallabies will again be seen, hopping around in the Grand Arch and the Devil's Coach House.

All of those years ago, while I was having my first dinner in Caves House, it suddenly started thundering, even though the sun was still shining, and there were no storm-clouds.

58

But when I mentioned this to the waitress, she smiled and answered, "It does sound like thunder, doesn't it? But actually, it's the wallabies - masses of them - bounding down the hillside at the back of Caves House, because they know that this is the time when the kitchen hands are emptying out bucketfuls of scraps."

And sure enough, at that same time every day, the hills behind Caves House would start thundering and vibrating as thousands of wallabies came leaping down for their supper.

During the rest of the day, they were everywhere - all over the surrounding hills, and chasing about enjoying themselves amongst the great strewn boulders in the Devil's Coach House and the Grand Arch. In fact, in the Grand Arch especially, the rocks were all brightly polished and slippery-smooth, from the constant friction of wallaby tails and feet.

Although they were timid, they didn't seem actually afraid of human visitors to Jenolan, at that time. But when one of them gently sidled up to me one day and nibbled a piece of toast as I held it out to him, this became my own special moment of wallaby magic.

Then, there was Billy, the little woman who worked in the kiosk. She had twinkling eyes and goldy-white curls, and her face kept wrinkling itself up with mischief. She also had bracelets that jingled with every movement - and I never saw her without one of Jenolan's beautiful, brightly coloured birds perched on her shoulder.

As for the caves themselves - fairylands of crystalline wonder - they were like another world altogether: silent and secret through aeons of time before human beings discovered them. And it's possible that the beginning of them goes back hundreds of millions of years.

To me, they seemed like a family - closely related, yet each individually different. Jubilee, for instance, all white and rosy like a bride, so different from the grim ruggedness of her brother Lucas.

Back then when I first visited Jenolan, there were two Imperial Caves - Right and Left. Years later, Left Imperial was renamed, and became Chifley.   In spite of this, when Thel met her, Imperial Cave herself was still very much thinking "right" and "left" - as you've discovered.

Also, all of those years ago, I was able to visit Skeleton Cave. But now, it's "off limits", because the bones that it guards are those of an aborigine, who evidently fell to his death there, about twenty thousand years ago - and it just doesn't seem right for people to stand around staring at them. That explains the strange feeling that Thel got when she and Wally came near to them.

As a personality, the Temple of Baal is a real mixture, perhaps because he has a dragon's throat (a very ancient river-bed), as well as two magnificent angels' wings - one white, the other russet - and more helictites than any other cave in Jenolan. And of course, helictites - or heligoblins, as Thel knew them - are quite irresponsible. You never know what they're going to do next. Yet they too, like stalactites, stalagmites, shawls, and so on, come about by the slow, slow dripping of water - which makes them quite difficult to explain.

Orient, on the other hand, is all dignity, splendour, and good behaviour, with caverns like palatial halls, and the most wonderful collection of richly coloured shawls, and of course the Pillar of Hercules, where Thel had such a frightening experience.

When we ourselves try to remember something that happened even a few days ago, we quite often get it wrong.

So it wouldn't be surprising if old Lucas's memories

weren't always accurate, considering that they reach back over millions of years. His famous column might, indeed, have been broken suddenly by an earthquake, but it might also have happened more slowly - the result of gradual earth movements. I'm sure, however, that neither Thel nor any of his Caves family would ever succeed in convincing him of that.

The guides, who show visitors through the caves in separate groups, are always very friendly and knowledgeable. But during my own first visit there, one of them in particular - the head guide, who wore white stars on his lapels - was somehow different. His name was Mr Bradley, and he knew the caves better than anyone else there, for he had helped with the exploration of them, and had even cut some of the thousands of steps which now make it so easy for people to walk through them. Otherwise, we might still have to be swinging ourselves down into caverns on ropes, or - like Thel - slippery-sliding into goodness-knows-what.

Once, after going through one of the caves with Mr White-Star Bradley as guide, I stood talking with him for a few moments in the Grand Arch, about the grandeur and marvel of Jenolan, and especially about the miraculous beauty of the caves.

"Yes indeed," he answered. Then, as though he were letting me into a very special secret, he added quietly, "And all of it the work of tiny waterdrops - and of Great Old Age."

Great Old Age. Three simple enough words, yet they kept coming back and back into my mind for the rest of the day, almost as if they connected with a special sort of "Something" that I'd felt hovering in the air, silently and invisibly, ever since arriving there. Then suddenly, just as I was about to go to sleep that night, the truth about them dawned on me - and startled me awake again.

Why, of course! The caves of Jenolan were pure magic, weren't they? Magic, enchantment, wizardry. And - as Mr White-Star Bradley undoubtedly well knew, Great Old Age was none other than the wizard himself. The Wizard of Jenolan.

Jenolan Caves

JUBILEE CAVE

RIGHT IMPERIAL C

UNDER
RIV

LUCAS CAVE

pinnacle

CATHEDRAL

pool of
CERBERUS

JENOLAN
RIVER

UNDERGROUND RIVER